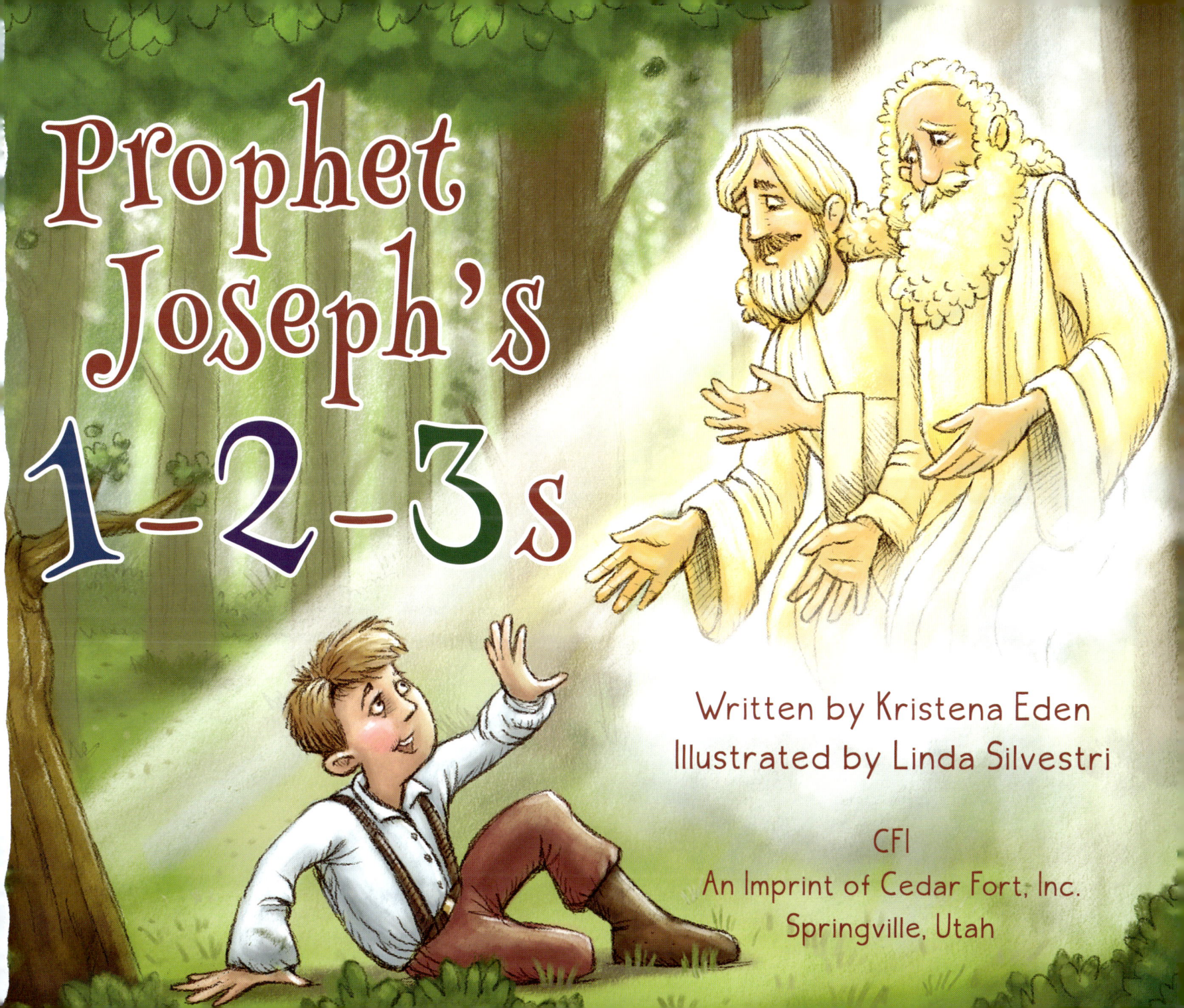

Our Heritage: A Brief History of The Church of Jesus Christ of Latter-day Saints
(Salt Lake City: The Church of Jesus Christ of Latter-day Saints, 1996).
Hereafter referred to as *Our Heritage*.

Teachings of Presidents of the Church: Joseph Smith (Salt Lake City: The Church of
Jesus Christ of Latter-day Saints, 2007). Hereafter referred to as *T of JS*.

Text © 2016 Kristena Eden
Illustrations © 2016 Linda Silvestri
All rights reserved.

No part of this book may be reproduced in any form whatsoever, whether by graphic, visual, electronic, film, microfilm, tape recording, or any other means, without prior written permission of the publisher, except in the case of brief passages embodied in critical reviews and articles.

This is not an official publication of The Church of Jesus Christ of Latter-day Saints. The opinions and views expressed herein belong solely to the author and do not necessarily represent the opinions or views of Cedar Fort, Inc. Permission for the use of sources, graphics, and photos is also solely the responsibility of the author.

ISBN 13: 978-1-4621-1949-3

Published by CFI, an imprint of Cedar Fort, Inc.
2373 W. 700 S., Springville, UT 84663
Distributed by Cedar Fort, Inc., www.cedarfort.com

Library of Congress Control Number: 2016946271

Cover and interior layout design by Shawnda T. Craig
Cover design © 2016 Cedar Fort, Inc.
Edited by Chelsea Holdaway

Printed in the United States of America

10 9 8 7 6 5 4 3 2 1

Printed on acid-free paper

I dedicate this book to all the people in
my life who have believed in me.
I also dedicate this book to my family
whom I believe in deeply.
—Kristena

To my mom, for always believing in me.
—Linda

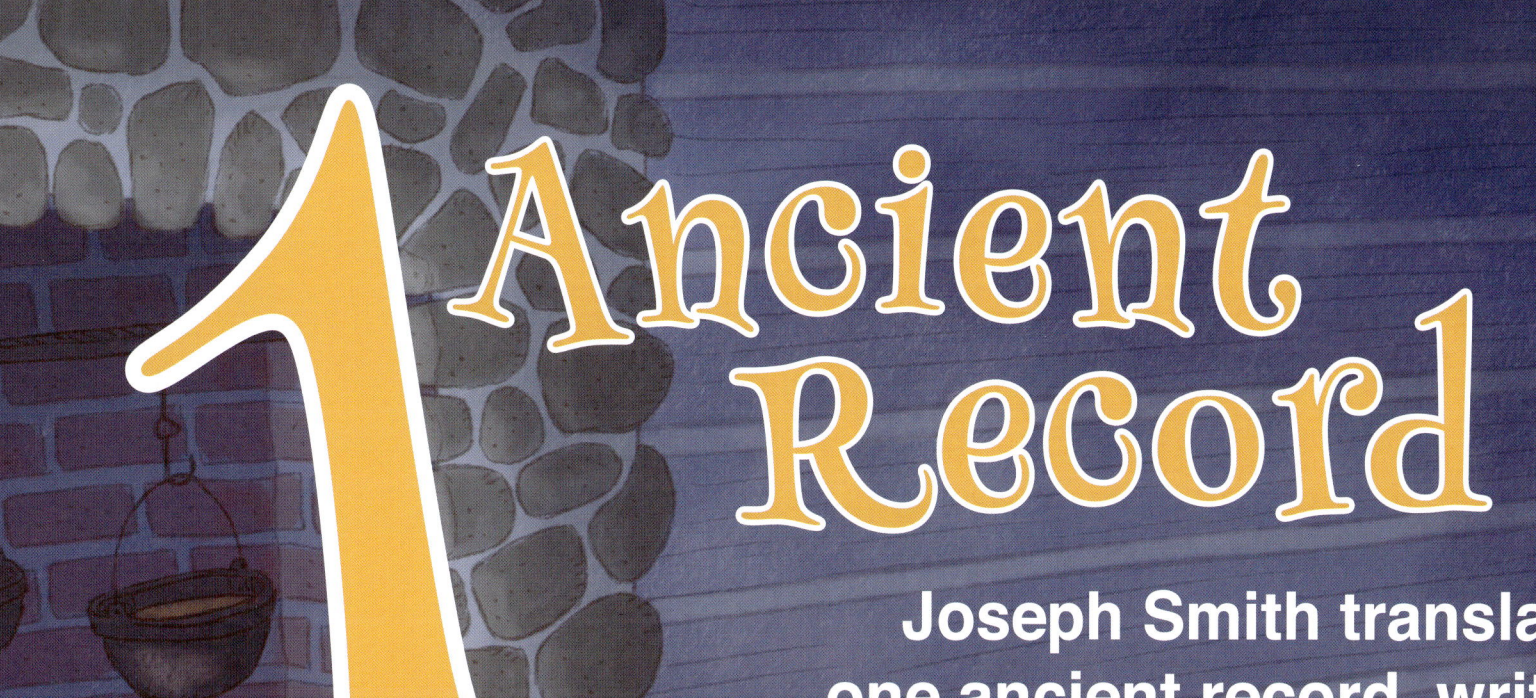

1 Ancient Record

Joseph Smith translated one ancient record, written on thin **PLATES OF GOLD**.

Joseph's translation is what we know as the **BOOK OF MORMON**, which teaches us more about **JESUS CHRIST**.

D&C 1:29

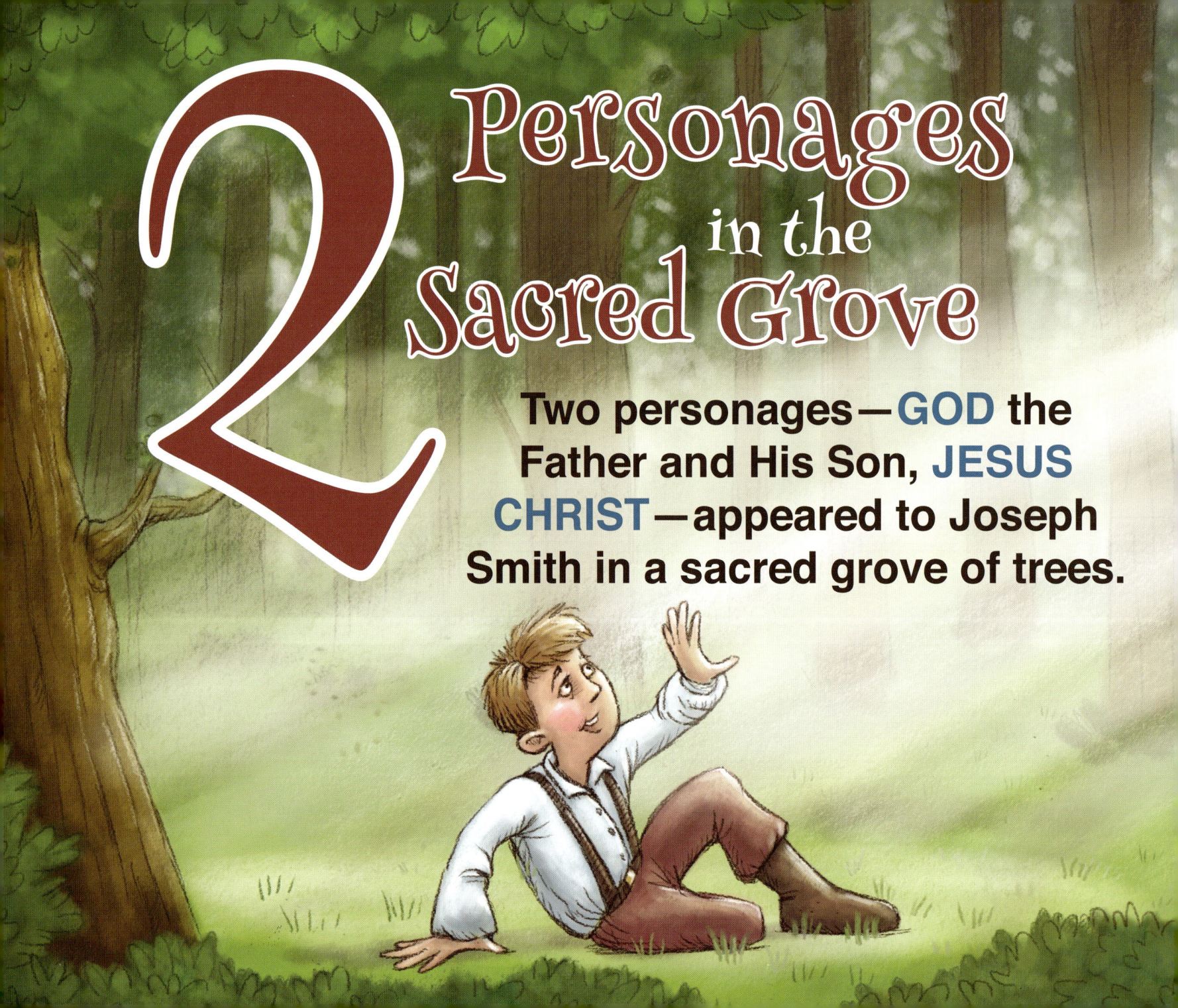

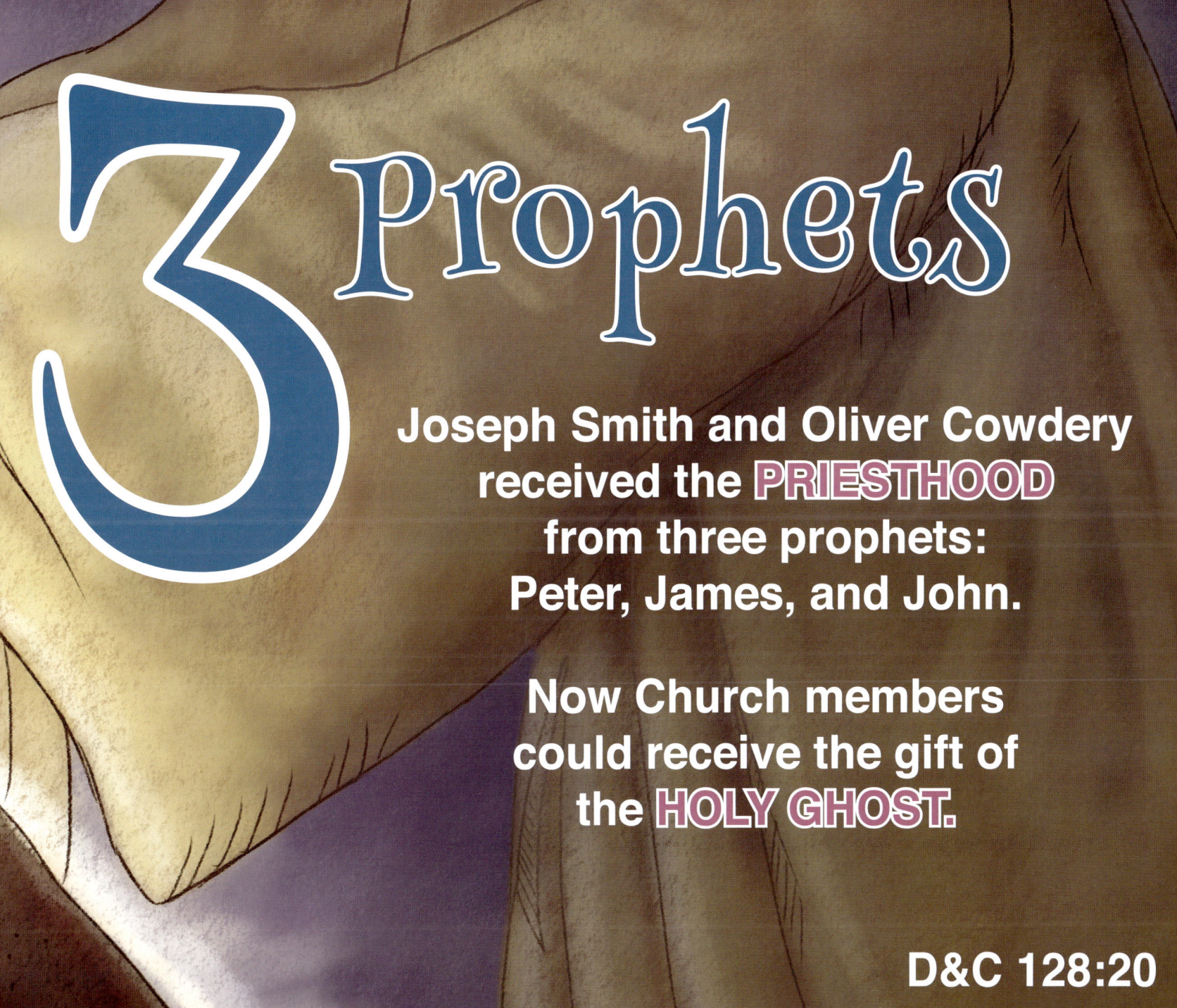

4 Visits from Moroni

An **ANGEL** named Moroni visited Joseph Smith four times, giving him instructions on what to do and where to find the **GOLD PLATES**.

T of JS, B of M intro

5 Trips to the Hill Cumorah

Joseph Smith walked to the Hill Cumorah five times.

On his last trip, the **ANGEL MORONI** instructed him to take the **GOLD PLATES** back to his home and begin translating them.

T of JS, B of M intro

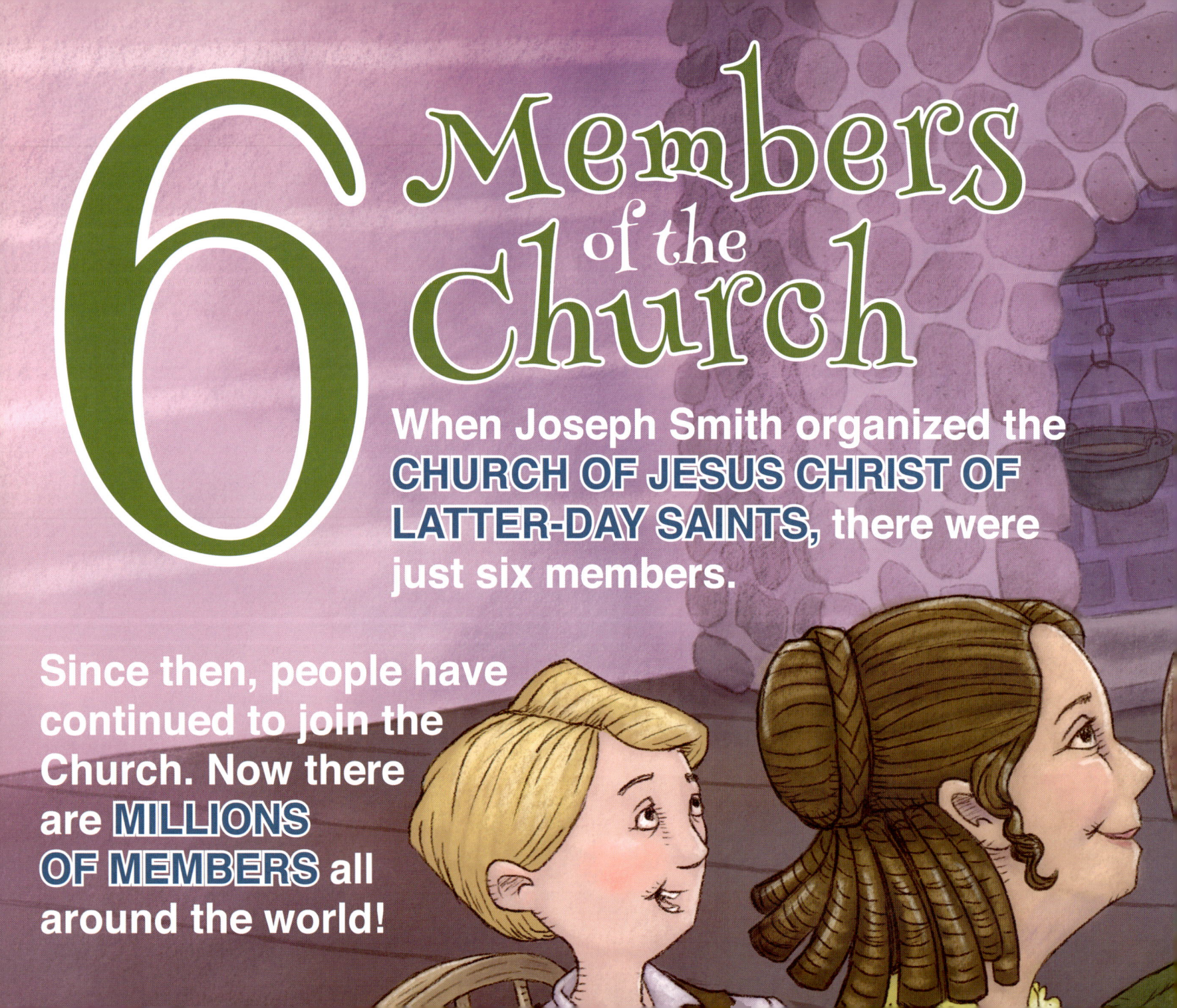

6 Members of the Church

When Joseph Smith organized the CHURCH OF JESUS CHRIST OF LATTER-DAY SAINTS, there were just six members.

Since then, people have continued to join the Church. Now there are MILLIONS OF MEMBERS all around the world!

During the translation of the **BOOK OF MORMON**, Joseph Smith and his family needed some food. Without being asked, a kind man named Joseph Knight Sr. brought food to help. As we **SERVE OTHERS** and strive to keep the **COMMANDMENTS**, **HEAVENLY FATHER** often **SENDS PEOPLE** to **HELP** us.

Our Heritage, p. 9

10 Years of Truths

From the FIRST VISION to the printing of the BOOK OF MORMON, ten years had gone by.

During these wonderful years, Joseph Smith and the new Church members **LEARNED MANY PRECIOUS TRUTHS.**

Because of this **RESTORATION,** we have the **BLESSINGS** of temples, priesthood power, and living prophets.

T of JS

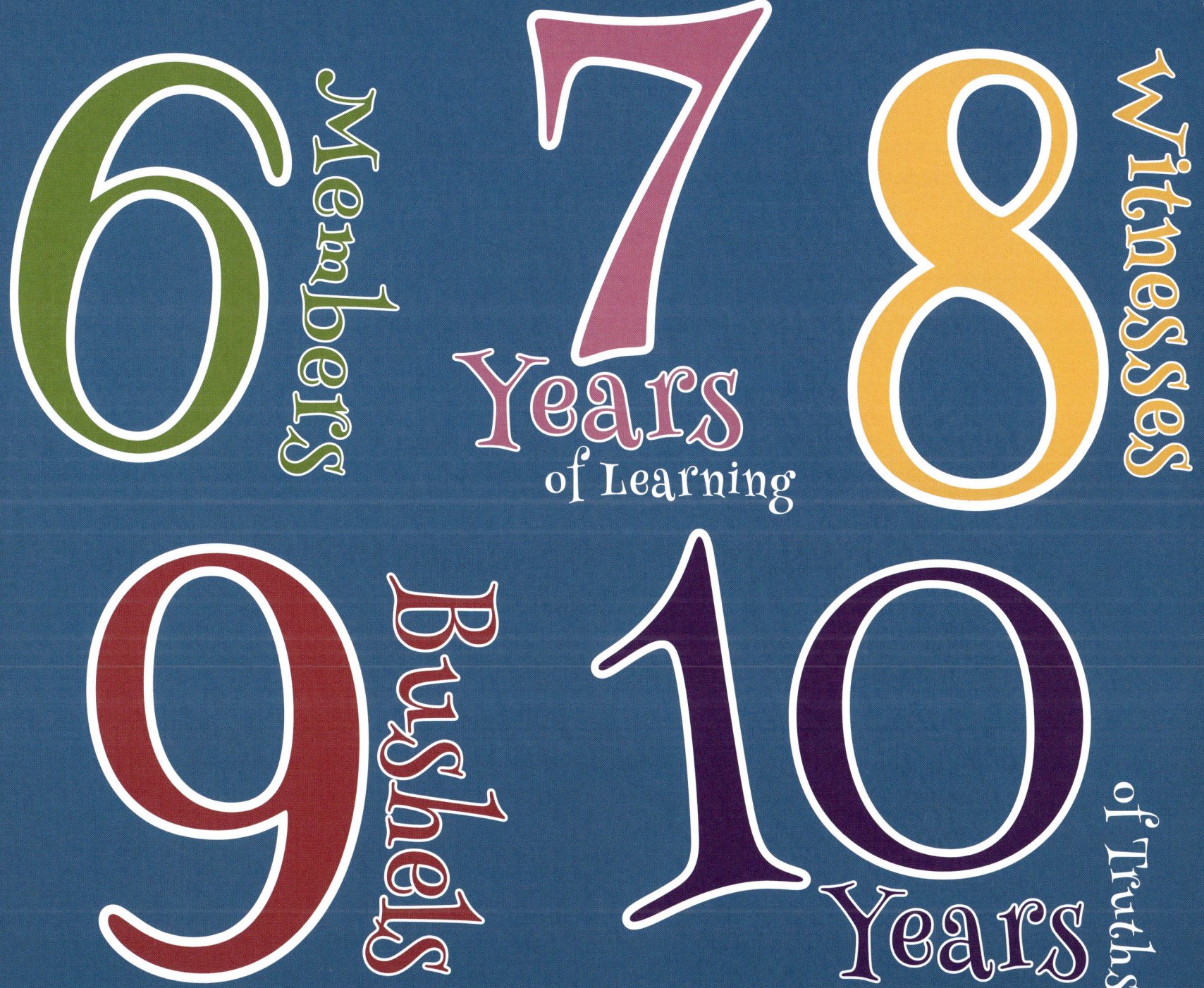

The Author

Kristena Eden was born in Oceanside, California, but she grew up around the world because her dad worked for the military. She has a degree in child development and was the owner and operator of Discovery Preschool. She also taught private kindergarten.

Kristena is the mother of six kids and the grandmother of eleven. She currently lives with her husband and two dogs in Bluffdale, Utah, where she spends time developing her artistic talents with painting and pottery. Visit Kristena at www.kristenasfineart.com and at thewritebook.com, " 'The Write Book' Inspiration Found Here."

The Illustrator

Linda Silvestri is an illustrator who lives in Southern California, in a wee ranch-style house that she shares with Ignatz, a cranky calico, and her lovely husband, Tom. Her illustrations use a dash of traditional line work with generous doses of digital painting, peppered with plenty of whimsy. Linda loves her job and plays well with others. See more from Linda at www.lindasilvestri.com.

Scan to visit
kristenasfineart.com

Scan to visit
thewritebook.com

Scan to visit
lindasilvestri.com